The Missing Heiress Mystery

Elaine Pageler

High Noon Books
Novato, California

Cover Design and Interior Illustrations: Tina Cash

International Standard Book Number: 1-57128-063-4

0 9 8 7 6 5 4 3 2 1
2 1 0 9 8 7 6 5 4 3

You'll enjoy all the High Noon Books. Write for
a free full list of titles.

Contents

1 Good News 1

2 Lola's Story 7

3 The Plot Thickens.............................15

4 A New Heiress....................................22

5 Following Clues...................................29

6 The Real Proof....................................34

7 Uncle Ike 41

CHAPTER 1

Good News

Brad Jones looked at Meg Green. He thought she would want to talk about their Riddle Street story. But Meg didn't. Instead she looked at the front page of the News.

"What's she reading?" Brad wanted to know.

Brad rolled his chair to her desk. Then he looked over her shoulder. The story told about F.P. Tate. The man had died. His granddaughter was his only heir. No one knew where she was.

Lola Tate had been missing for twelve years.

"Poor Mr. Tate," Meg sighed.

"He wasn't poor. F.P. Tate owned banks and stores. He was a very rich man," Brad said.

"So what? He didn't have a family. That makes him poor," Meg told him.

Brad frowned and rolled his chair back to his desk. Why did he have to work with Meg? She argued about everything.

Just then the phone rang. It was their boss, Mr. Ross. He wanted to see them right away. Brad rushed up the stairs and Meg followed.

Mr. Ross met them at the door. He seemed excited. "Come in, Brad and Meg. I want you to meet Hal Craig," he said.

A man stood near the desk. His tanned face looked about fifty. He flashed them a smile and held out his hand. "So this is the Riddle Street team," he said.

Mr. Ross nodded. "Meg does the writing. Brad takes the pictures. They're tops at doing a story," he told him.

"That's what I need," Hal Craig said.

Mr. Ross turned to Brad and Meg. "Hal was F.P. Tate's lawyer. He has very good news. F.P.'s granddaughter, Lola, has been found," he told them.

"That's great!" Meg said.

"Where's she been for the last twelve years?" Brad wanted to know.

Hal Craig smiled. "Lola will tell you her story. The News will announce it tomorrow. But I want you to write a longer story. People will want to know more about her," he said.

"When do we start?" Meg asked.

"Can you come now? Lola is at my office," Hal Craig said.

Brad got his camera. Meg took her notebook. Moments later they drove down Riddle Street with Hal Craig. He took them to the tenth floor of a tall building. A sign was on the door. It said, "Craig Law Firm."

A man sat at the desk inside. He seemed about Hal's age. He looked up as they came in.

"This is Stubbs," Hal told them.

Stubbs smiled at them. "We're glad you're writing about Miss Tate. The poor girl has been through so much. I'm glad she's been found at last," he said.

"Stubbs has been here for years. Ask him, if you need anything," Hal said.

Then Hal pointed to a room with a glass window. It held a big table and chairs. "That's the best place to meet. You can wait here. I'll go to my office and get Lola," he said.

Brad and Meg went inside. They could see Hal's office through the window.

Soon the door opened and Hal entered. A young woman about Meg's age followed him. She had long red hair.

"Here's the heiress," Brad said.

Meg stared at her. "That looks like Tilly Mock! We were roommates at summer camp. Yes, I think it's her," she gasped.

Brad frowned at Meg. She must be mistaken. "When was that?" he demanded.

"It was eight years ago," Meg told him.

"People change in eight years. And you can't remember that long," Brad told her.

"She has the same red hair," Meg said.

"Lots of girls have red hair. Lola just looks a lot like her," Brad argued.

Meg sighed. "I guess you're right. What would Tilly be doing here? But that girl does remind me of her," she told him.

CHAPTER 2

Lola's Story

Brad had been talking to Meg. Now he looked back at Lola Tate. She walked toward them. Her eyes were fixed on Meg. There was a strange look on her face. Was Meg right?

Now Lola turned her head and looked at him. Brad saw how pretty she was. That strange look went away. She's just tired, Brad thought.

Hal Craig led the young woman to a chair. "Lola, this is Brad and Meg," he said.

Lola's face broke into a big smile. "Thank

you for doing my story," she said.

Brad smiled, too. He reached for his camera.

Mr. Craig put a hand on Brad's arm. "Don't take any close shots of her face," he said.

Brad frowned. "Why not?" he asked.

"Lola will have lots of money. It's safer that people don't know what she looks like," Hal said.

That made sense to Brad. "Don't worry. I won't take close-ups," he told Lola.

Meg pulled out her notebook. "Tell us your story. Where were you born?" she asked.

"She was born here. Her parents moved to Mexico when she was two," Hal Craig said.

Lola nodded. "I don't remember living

here. But I remember Mexico. We lived there for eight years. One day my dad told me we were going back to the U.S. We would live with Grandfather. I was surprised. Mom and Dad never talked about him. I didn't know I had a grandfather," she said.

"Didn't you know F.P. was rich?" Brad asked.

Lola shook her head. "There wasn't time to talk then. Dad said he'd tell me about him on the plane. He gave me this box," she said.

She handed them a box. It held two things. One was F.P.'s picture with his name on it. The other was her old passport. It was badly scorched.

"The next morning we got on the plane. The sky was filled with clouds. We started over

9

Lola handed them a small box.

high mountains. Dad had just started talking about Grandfather when we crashed," Lola said.

Hal Craig cut in. "Lola was ten. The plane crashed in steep mountains. It was found a month later. Everyone was killed but Lola. She was missing. They searched for her. But the land was too rough," he said.

"Some Mexican peasants found me. I still had the box. And my arm had a bad cut," Lola told them. She showed them a jagged scar on her left arm.

Lola went on. "The peasants took me to their village. It was high in the mountains. No one ever came there," she said.

"Have you lived there ever since?" Brad

asked the young woman.

"Lola couldn't have. Her English is too good," Meg said.

Lola shot her a glance and smiled. "That's right. I've lived in the U.S. for eight years. Two hikers came to the village. They were from the U.S. I showed them Grandfather's picture. They knew him. They said they'd tell Grandfather. I waited. But he never came to get me," Lola said.

A sad look covered Hal's face. "The men had to hike out. That took a while. They flew here with the news. F.P. was so happy. But he was too old to make the trip. So he sent me. Lola was gone when I got there," he said.

"I thought no one was coming. Then another hiker came. He took me to his sister in the U.S.," Lola said.

"Did you go to Iowa?" Meg asked.

Lola shook her head. "No, Uncle Ike took me to a ranch in Utah. I was fifteen. I've lived there ever since," she said.

"Did you try to find your grandfather?" Brad asked.

"Yes, but I had no address. There are lots of Tates in the U.S. Then last week F.P. Tate's death was on TV. They showed his picture. I knew he was my grandfather," Lola told them

"Lola phoned us. I knew her story was true when I saw the locket around her neck," Hal said.

"Why is that?" Meg asked.

"F.P. gave it to her on her first birthday. I was there. Now, that's enough for today. Let's meet at F.P.'s mansion in the morning," Hal said.

Brad and Meg started back to the News. They talked over this story.

"Lola still reminds me of Tilly. That's why I asked about Iowa. She lived there," Meg said.

"Did Tilly have a scar?" Brad asked.

Meg shook her head.

"The girl has her passport and her locket. She also has a picture of F.P. What more proof do you want?" Brad asked.

For once, Meg looked unsure of herself. "I don't know," she said.

CHAPTER 3

The Plot Thickens

Brad worked at the photo lab the next morning. He was doing Lola's pictures.

"Knock, knock," came a sound from the door.

It was Meg. "Hurry up. We need to be at the mansion in an hour," she yelled.

Brad glanced at his watch. "The mansion is ten minutes away," he called.

"We have to pick up Amy Worth," Meg yelled.

Brad popped his head out of the door. "Who is Amy Worth?" he asked.

"Amy Worth was F.P. Tate's maid for years. She remembers Lola," Meg said.

"I don't believe it. You're still trying to prove Lola is Tilly Mock," Brad snapped.

Meg gave him a sweet smile. "Who said anything about Tilly Mock? I'm just getting the facts. There's something odd about Lola's story. Why didn't her dad and mom tell her about F.P. Tate?" she asked.

Brad thought that was strange, too. He closed the lab. And they drove over to get Amy Worth.

The old woman was waiting for them. She wore an apron over her dress. "Miss Lola may need some help," she told them.

Brad drove on to the mansion. Hal Craig's car was already there. They parked near it. Then Brad, Meg, and Amy walked to the door.

Hal opened it. His smile turned to a frown. "Why hello, Amy. What are you doing here?" he asked.

"Meg asked me to come. She knew I would like to see Lola," Amy told him.

Hal smiled but he didn't seem happy. "Come in," he told them.

Lola came toward them. She stopped and stared at Amy. "I don't think I know you," she said.

Hal spoke up quickly. "This is Amy Worth. She was F.P.'s maid," he said.

"I knew you wouldn't remember me. But I did want to see you. Yes, you have the same red hair. I bet you still have that scar on your arm, too," Amy said.

Lola gave her a blank look. "A scar?" she asked.

Amy nodded. "You climbed up on a table when you were very small and fell on a vase. It cut your left arm," she told her.

Lola's blank stare changed to a smile. "Now I remember. There was a scar. But that was before the crash," she said.

Lola took off her jacket. She showed Amy her jagged scar. "The big scar covered the little scar," she told her.

Amy nodded. "F.P. really missed you and your parents. It's too bad about the big fight," she said.

"What fight?" Meg asked.

Hal Craig frowned. "I had hoped we wouldn't need to talk about this. But you better be told. Lola's dad worked for F.P. One day a million dollars was missing. Everything pointed to Lola's dad. He said he didn't take it. But F.P. didn't believe him," he said.

"So that's why we went to Mexico," Lola said.

Amy Worth nodded. "It's also why your parents didn't talk about your grandfather. Mr. Tate wouldn't talk about his son either. But I knew he missed him," she said.

Hal cut in. "A man confessed eight years later. He had taken the money. F.P. wrote his son and begged him to come home," Hal said.

"Then the crash happened. Mr. Tate always thought Lola was alive," Amy Worth added.

Brad got his camera. He took pictures.

"There's another picture you should have. The hiker took it of Lola. It's when she was living with the peasants. Stop by my office. Stubbs will give it to you. I'll take Amy home," Hal said.

So Brad and Meg stopped at the Craig Law office. They told Stubbs what they wanted. He found the picture for them.

"It isn't very clear," Meg said.

"Yes, but it's Lola. See her red hair and the jagged cut on her arm," Brad told her.

"I remember the day the men brought that picture. Lola Tate was alive. They knew where she was. I made a copy of their map for Hal. And he left the next day," Stubbs said.

Brad led the way back outside. "Are all your questions answered now?" he asked.

"There's just one thing. Did you see how Lola looks at me? I think she knows me, too," Meg told him.

Brad recalled the look on Lola's face. It was when she first saw Meg. No, Lola was the heiress. There was too much proof.

CHAPTER 4

A New Heiress

The next morning Brad and Meg worked on the Lola Tate story. Meg always liked writing. But today she was glum.

Then the phone rang. It was Sergeant Ward. "I hear you two are writing about the Tate heiress," he said.

"That's right," Brad told him.

"Then you should come down to the station. We have a girl there. She claims to be Lola Tate, too," Sergeant Ward said.

Brad couldn't believe it. He hung up and told Meg what the sergeant had said.

Meg jumped up. A big grin spread across her face. "I knew it. That other girl is Tilly. Come on. Let's go," she said.

Brad grabbed his camera and chased after her. "How do you know this new girl isn't a fake?" he asked.

Sergeant Ward was glad to see them. He led them to a room.

A red-haired girl sat inside. From the door she looked a bit like Lola. But she didn't when they got closer. Her old slacks and shirt hung on her. She was very thin. There were dark circles under her eyes.

A red-haired girl sat inside. She was very thin with dark circles under her eyes.

"This is Brad and Meg from the News. Tell them your name," Sergeant Ward said.

"My name is Lola Tate. And my grandfather was F.P. Tate. These people don't believe me. But he really was," the girl said. Tears showed in her eyes.

Meg put an arm around her. "I want to hear your story," she said.

Brad turned to Sergeant Ward. "Can we order food in? Meg and I haven't had breakfast. Let's get some for this girl, too," he said.

Sergeant Ward smiled. "I think that's a good idea," he said.

The girl started to say something. Meg stopped her. "The News will pay," she said.

The food came. They ate and talked. Breakfast seemed to help the girl. Some color came back into her cheeks.

The first part of her story was like the other Lola's. Both girls told about the village. They told of the hikers and waiting for Grandfather to come. But their story changed with Uncle Ike. This girl just called him Ike. He was to bring her back. But Ike didn't take her to the U.S. He took her somewhere else in Mexico.

"Did he leave you there?" Brad asked.

The girl nodded. "Ike took me to some people. They had a shop. He told them to keep me there. I would work for them," she said.

"You were only fifteen," Meg said.

"That's right. It took me two years. But I escaped. I worked my way north. A family hired me as their maid. They brought me to the U.S. After a year, they went back. And I stayed here," the girl told them

"What did you do then?" Meg asked.

"I did odd jobs. No one would give me a good job. I couldn't prove I was from the U.S. Ike had stolen all my things," the girl said.

"What things?" Brad asked.

"He took my locket and my box. It had my passport and a picture of Grandfather inside. I begged him to give them back. He said I didn't need them. But he did," the girl said.

Meg shot Brad a glance. Then she turned

back to the girl, "Do you have a scar on your left arm?" she asked.

The girl nodded. She pulled up her sleeve. Brad glanced at her arm. It had a jagged scar.

"For years I have searched for Grandfather. Then I saw his picture in a newspaper. It said he had died and Lola Tate had been found. That's a lie. I came to tell you so. The bus ride took all my money," the girl said.

"Do you have any proof that you're Lola Tate?" Brad asked.

The girl's face looked sad. She shook her head. "No, I don't. All I have is my story," she told them.

CHAPTER 5

Following Clues

Brad and Meg came out of the room. Sergeant Ward was waiting for them.

"What do you think?" he asked.

"I think she's Lola Tate," Meg told him.

Sergeant Ward looked surprised. "This girl has no proof at all," he said.

"Meg has a crazy idea. She thinks the first girl is a fake," Brad told him.

"Yes, I think she's Tilly Mock," Meg said.

"Who's Tilly Mock?" Sergeant Ward asked.

"Eight years ago I went to summer camp. Tilly Mock and I were roommates for two weeks. We weren't really good friends. But we spent a lot of time together. I wrote a play for the camp show. Tilly starred in it. She was a good actress. After camp she went back home to Iowa. That's where she lived. I wrote her once. But she didn't answer," Meg told them.

Brad turned to Sergeant Ward. "They were fourteen at the time. Meg can't be sure the girl is Tilly," he said.

Meg pushed out her chin. "There's something else, too. This girl told us of the locket, picture, and passport. How did she know about them?" she asked.

Brad nodded. "That's true. She couldn't have read about them. Our story hasn't come out yet," he added.

Sergeant Ward reached for his phone. "We need to talk to the first Lola Tate," he said.

An hour later, the first Lola walked into the station. She looked angry. "What's the meaning of this? Of course, I'm Lola Tate,' she said.

Sergeant Ward led her into the next room. He pointed to the second Lola sitting there.

"This girl has never met you. Still she told us all about your locket, passport, and picture of F.P. Tate. She claims they were stolen. Maybe she's right. How else could she know about them?" Sergeant Ward asked.

31

The first Lola's worried look changed. Now she smiled. "That's because I showed them to her. One summer she worked on my aunt's ranch in Utah," she said.

"That's not true!" exclaimed the other girl.

"She has a scar. It looks just like yours," Meg said.

The first Lola smiled again. "Yes, it happened that summer. She fell off a horse," she told them.

The other girl jumped out of her chair. "She's lying! I've never been to Utah in my life. My arm was hurt in a crash. It was in Mexico. Everyone died but me," she sobbed.

Meg went over. She put an arm around her.

Sergeant Ward turned to the first Lola. "What's your aunt's phone number and address? I want to check your story," he said.

She gave it to him. And he stalked out of the room. Soon he came back.

"Her story checks out," he told them.

"Of course, her aunt would lie. She's in on the plot," Meg said.

"Also, I called the high school in her town. A Lola Tate went there. She came when she was fifteen. I think this must be the real Lola Tate," Sergeant Ward told them.

The first Lola headed to the door. She stopped a minute and grinned at Meg. "Come to the mansion for tea sometime," she said.

CHAPTER 6

The Real Proof

Meg stormed down the street. "Did you hear Tilly Mock? She almost laughed in my face. At least Sergeant Ward agreed to keep the new girl for a day. We can do more checking. I'm sure she's the real Lola Tate," she said.

"I am, too. Maybe it's because the girl seems so alone. And that horse story can't be true. That's why I took a close-up picture of Tilly today. It might help us," Brad told her.

Brad went straight to the lab. He brought

the finished picture to Meg.

She faxed it to the high school in Utah. The answer came back. Yes, this was Lola Tate.

Next Meg phoned the high school in Iowa. It was where Tilly went to school.

A woman answered. "Yes, a Tilly Mock did go to school here for a while. But she and her family moved away," she said.

Meg faxed the picture to the woman.

"It looks like our picture. But I'm not sure. Our last school picture was when she was fourteen," the woman said.

Meg smiled at Brad. "Tilly Mock moved from Iowa. That must have been after summer camp. She shows up a year later in Utah. But now she calls herself Lola Tate," she said.

"Where was she for a year?" Brad asked.

"I think she was somewhere getting that scar. A doctor did it for her," Meg said.

Brad nodded. "Ike must have taken a picture of Lola's scar. Both girls spoke of him. So he's real. One girl said he was another hiker. The other said he was sent by F.P. Tate," he said.

Meg frowned. "Hal Craig was sent by him." She stopped and stared at Brad. "Could Hal be Ike?" she gasped.

"He was in the village," Brad pointed out.

"Let's go to the Craig Law office. We might learn something," Meg said.

Stubbs looked up when they walked in.

"May I help you?" he asked.

"You were here when Hal went to Mexico. How long was he gone?" Brad asked.

"Mr. Craig thought he would be back in a month. But he took longer. He closed the office. I got free time with pay," Stubbs told them.

Hal Craig came out of his office. There was a frown on his face. "Why are you here? Isn't your story done?" he asked.

"A new girl is at the police station. She claims to be Lola Tate. Wouldn't you like to talk to her?" Meg asked.

"No, I wouldn't. She's a fake. We have the real Lola. I've seen proof of that," Hal said. He walked back to his office and slammed the door.

Stubbs tried to smooth things over. "Mr. Craig has always felt guilty about Lola. There was a mix-up with his ticket. And he had to stay over a few days. Or he would have been to the village on time. Lola and Uncle Ike left one day before he got there," he told them.

Brad and Meg left. They went back to the station. Lola might recall something more. It might help them.

Lola was glad to talk. "Yes, Ike did take pictures of my arm. But I didn't know why," she said.

"He gave them to a doctor. He made a scar on Tilly's arm. It looked just like yours," Meg told her.

Lola pulled up her sleeve.
Above the jagged scar was a smaller one.

The sun streamed through the window. It was in Brad's face. He reached for the shade. But it was too high. He started to climb up on the nearby table. Then he could reach it.

"No! You could get hurt," Lola shouted.

"Why did you say that? Did you fall off a table?" Brad asked.

"I don't know," Lola said.

"Amy Worth said you did. You were very young. Let's see your arm again," Brad said.

Lola pulled up her sleeve. Above the jagged scar was a smaller one.

"There's our proof. It's the scar Amy spoke of. Ike didn't see this scar. It's much lighter than the other one," Brad told them.

CHAPTER 7

Uncle Ike

Brad and Meg showed Sergeant Ward Lola's proof. Also, they told him Hal must be Ike.

Sergeant Ward drove Brad, Meg, and Lola to the Tate mansion. Hal Craig's car was parked in front.

"That's good. We'll arrest both of them at the same time," he said.

A maid opened the door. Sergeant Ward pushed past her. Tilly and Hal sat inside. They were shocked to see Sergeant Ward.

Hal jumped up. "What's the meaning of this?" he asked.

"You're under arrest, Tilly Mock," Sergeant Ward told her.

Tilly pushed her nose in the air. "I'm Lola Tate. I have proof. Don't I, Hal?" she asked.

"Ike is under arrest, too," Sergeant Ward told her.

Lola had been standing with Brad and Meg. Now she rushed to Sergeant Ward. "That's not Ike. I've never seen this man before," she said.

That shocked Brad. He and Meg had been so sure.

"And she's not Lola Tate. Let's see her proof," Tilly snapped.

At least Brad was sure of that. "Show them your arm, Lola," he said.

"Take a good look.Remember what Amy told us," Meg added.

Hal's face turned white. "There are two scars. Oh, my dear, you are the real Lola Tate!" he said.

Then he turned toward the kitchen. "Stubbs come out here. We have great news," he called.

The door opened. Stubbs came out. He had food in his hands.

"That's Ike!" Lola exclaimed.

Stubbs started running. But Sergeant Ward caught him. "You and Tilly Mock are going to jail," he told him.

Meg looked at Brad. "Of course. Stubbs was there when the men came. He saw the picture. It reminded him of his niece in Iowa. There was a way to get F.P.'s money," she said.

Brad nodded. "Stubbs made two maps. One for Hal. The other was for himself," he added.

Hal Craig agreed. "Stubbs got my ticket. That's why there was a mix-up. He needed time to get to Lola first. But it didn't work. Thanks to you two, F.P.'s real granddaughter will live in his house," he said.

Lola turned to Brad and Meg. "Thank you. Will you come visit me?" she asked.

"How about dinner Friday night?" Brad said with a smile.